Treasury of Princess Stories

igloobooks

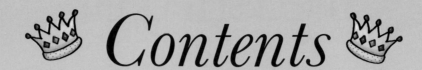 # Contents

This igloo book belongs to:

....

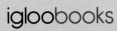

Published in 2013
by Igloo Books Ltd
Cottage Farm
Sywell
NN6 0BJ
www.igloobooks.com

SHE001 0713
2 4 6 8 10 9 7 5 3
ISBN 978-0-85780-775-5

Illustrated by Kimberley Scott
Written by Elizabeth Dale

Printed and manufactured in China

👑 Contents 👑

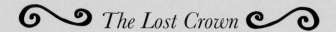
The Lost Crown

It was a lovely, sunny morning in the Little Kingdom. At the palace, the king was in a very bad mood. "Where's my crown?!" he bellowed. "I can't find it anywhere!"

The queen sighed. "Oh, no," she said. "The king is always losing his crown. Now, everyone in the palace will have to stop what they were doing and search for it."

The queen sent her maid to wake Princess Poppy. After much grumbling, Poppy came downstairs. "I'm so sorry," said the queen, when they met in the corridor. "You know how your father will be if we don't find his crown. We must help to look for it."

Princess Poppy gave a weary sigh and started looking. She searched in cupboards and drawers and even under her father's pillow. All over the palace, it seemed that the servants were running around, frantically searching everywhere for the lost crown. Every single corridor echoed with footsteps and the sound of clattering and banging. Everything possible was moved, peered under and looked inside, but the crown was nowhere to be found.

Princess Poppy put her hands over her ears. "What a terrible din!" she cried. "It's giving me a headache." The queen insisted that they keep searching. However, as soon as her mother's back was turned, Poppy rushed outside and ran along the path that led to the rose garden. Suddenly, she heard her mother's voice calling, "Poppy, come back here, this instant!"

It's far too nice to be inside, thought Poppy. She wanted to play and enjoy the sunshine, not search for Daddy's silly old crown. Poppy quickly ran into the rose garden. However, when she saw that her mother had nearly caught up with her, Poppy tripped and tumbled backwards. "Oh, dear!" she cried.

Princess Poppy landed on something soft. "Ouch!" cried a boy's voice. "Watch out!"
"Who are you?" said Princess Poppy.
"I'm Ned," replied the boy. "I'm the farmer's son and I'm trying to get out of looking for the king's lost crown. I've come here to hide."

Princess Poppy smiled at Ned. "I'm hiding, too," she said. Suddenly, Poppy heard her mother coming closer. "Quick, run!" she cried. She and Ned dashed from behind the bush and ran along the path.

"This way," said Ned, grabbing Poppy's hand. He led them through a hidden opening in the hedge. Poppy just managed to squeeze through. With the queen calling behind them, they ran, laughing and giggling, right out of the palace gates.

"My Dad's farm is just over the fields," said Ned. "Would you like to see the animals?" "Yes, please," said Poppy.

First, Ned took Poppy to see a mare with her cute, little foal. "We can feed the hens, next, if you like?" he suggested and led Poppy across a big field, full of sheep. However, as Poppy followed him into the farmyard, she was so excited, she forgot to shut the gate.

Poppy was in the middle of feeding the chickens when there was loud bleating and baaing. "Oh, no," said Ned. "The sheep have escaped. We've got to get them back or my dad will be furious." Poppy felt terrible. It was all her fault. She was determined to help Ned catch the sheep.

Ned and Poppy chased the sheep all over the farmyard. There were sheep in the pigsty and sheep in the barn, trampling over flowerbeds, even peering through the kitchen window! Buckets went flying and jugs were overturned. Princess Poppy grabbed hold of a sheep and got her dress all covered in mud.

It took Ned and Poppy ages to get all the sheep back into the field. The last one was almost in when an angry voice shouted, "What on earth is going on?"
"Oh, no," whispered Ned. "It's Dad. Now I'm really in trouble." He grabbed Poppy's hand. "Come on. Run!"

Poppy and Ned ran, as fast as they could, over the fields towards the palace. Poppy suddenly noticed how muddy her dress was. "I can't let my parents see me like this," she cried and darted into the coach house. There was always water in there to clean the royal coaches. Maybe she could clean herself up a bit?

Suddenly, Poppy heard her mother and father outside. "Oh, no," she said. "Quick, hide!" With that, Polly jumped into the king's carriage. Ned followed and, as Poppy moved further in, she saw something gold glinting under the seat. It was the king's crown! "Poppy, I know you are in there. Come out at once!" said the queen, crossly.

Poppy and Ned emerged, looking very pleased. "I've found Daddy's crown!" shouted Poppy. The queen gasped when she saw her daughter's very muddy dress.

However, the king was so happy that his crown had been found, he offered Poppy a reward. "I'd like to play with Ned and wear jeans so that I can get muddy without ruining my dresses," she said. Ned's father, who had finally caught up with them, thought this was a very good idea. He liked the idea of having a royal princess on his farm.

Now, Princess Poppy would be able to have fun with Ned on the farm all the time. She was very happy and it was all thanks to her Dad's lost crown.

Princess Posy and the Magic Mirror

Princess Posy was the most spoilt princess in the whole world. Everyone thought so, except, of course, the king and queen. They thought she was the most perfectly wonderful little angel, ever. Posy had nappies made of silk, sheets made of velvet and her bed was so soft and bouncy, that when she jumped onto it, she bounced as high as the ceiling! All Posy had to do was point at something like a puppy wandering by, a pretty necklace or huge ice-cream and it was hers. Whatever Posy wanted, she got.

As Posy got older, her wishes grew more demanding. Poor Cook had to make a triple-layer, extra-squidgy, chocolate and marshmallow cake, at a moment's notice. The palace staff could hardly sleep for worrying what they'd be summoned to make next. Princess Posy would call on them day and night, but nothing they ever did seemed to be good enough for her.

Then, one day, Princess Posy heard a rumor about something incredible. Somewhere in the kingdom, was a magic mirror that granted every wish, instantly. "I want it," she told the king. "I want it NOW!"

"Find the magic mirror!" shouted the king to his men. "Quickly!"

So, the king's men saddled up their horses and rode far and wide, over mountains and rivers, stopping at every village and farm, asking, "Have you seen the magic mirror?"

Nobody knew anything about the mirror. The king's men went back to the palace empty-handed. When they got there, the princess shrieked, "I want that mirror and I want it, RIGHT NOW!"

So, the king's men continued searching, high and low. Eventually, in a little house, in a dark wood, they found a clever old witch, who had heard all about the princess. "I'll make a magic mirror fit for Princess Posy," she cackled.

Sometime later, back at the palace, the king handed Posy a brand new, golden mirror. She carried the beautiful mirror up to her room. Posy knew just what to wish for. "Magic Mirror," she commanded. "Give me a beautiful, diamond tiara." Then, Posy closed her eyes and something landed on her head.

The surprised princess opened her eyes and gazed in the mirror. It really was magic. There really was a tiara on her head and it was beautiful. "Hooray!" she cried, peering closer in the mirror. The diamonds were huge. However, Princess Posy's nose was suddenly huge, too! In fact, it was ENORMOUS!

Princess Posy was furious. She stomped off to bed, refusing to let anyone into her room. No one must see her nose, absolutely no one.

The next morning, Posy peered in her magic mirror. Her nose was still big and it looked awful. Posy dipped it in cold water and stuck it out the window. Whatever she tried, it didn't shrink. To distract herself, she grabbed her mirror. "Magic Mirror, give me a golden piano!" she commanded.

Suddenly, right before her eyes, a golden piano appeared. It was very beautiful. Posy looked back in her mirror, but gasped in horror. Her teeth had all gone wonky.

Every time Princess Posy picked up the mirror, the huge nose and ghastly teeth were still there. Why? She'd been pretty before she got the magic mirror. Had each wish made her uglier? Perhaps she should stop?

The trouble was, she couldn't. Princess Posy still wanted more. "Give me a beautiful horse!" she commanded the mirror. Just then, an elegant white stallion appeared. Posy stroked him, lovingly. "You're so beautiful," she sighed. The stallion gave her a look as though to say, "Well, you're not!"

Posy looked in her mirror again. Now her chin had sprouted a huge wart.

Maria, Posy's maid, couldn't believe her eyes. "What happened?" she asked.
"It's my magic mirror!" wailed Posy. "Every time I wish for something, I get uglier."
Maria picked up the magic mirror. "Let me have a go," she said. "Magic Mirror, please make everyone who is sad, feel happy," said Maria.

Suddenly, there was a commotion in the streets, outside the palace. People sang and cheered. "What's happened?" called Maria.
"We all feel so happy!" cried the people, jumping for joy. "We just want to dance and sing!"

"If you wish for good things for others, nothing bad will happen to you," said Maria.
"Really?" replied Posy. "I wish for good weather, so people can have parties outside."
Just then, a warm breeze wafted through the window.

20

Posy looked in the magic mirror. Her wart had gone. "I wish that anyone who is sick, feels better soon," said Posy. Suddenly, her teeth became white and straight. "Hurray," she said. "I wish that Maria has new shoes!"

Suddenly, Maria's tatty shoes became shiny, new ones and Posy's nose was small again. She took Maria's hand and together they ran outside to join the wonderful celebrations. Seeing everyone laughing and hugging made Posy happier than owning any of the things she had wished for.

From that day on, Princess Posy decided never to make unreasonable demands again. If she felt tempted, she knew that all she had to do was to take one look in her magic mirror.

21

Princess Marigold's Music

Princess Marigold was very excited. Today, at long last, was the day that her father, the king, had said that she could start to learn a musical instrument. She got up early and rushed into the music room. Marigold gazed around at the instruments that her brothers and sisters played so well. Finally, she'd be able to join them in royal concerts and make her parents proud of her. "I'll have a go on the drums," said Marigold. So, she sat down and began to play. *Bang, Bang, CRASH!*

The king and queen rushed into the music room. "What's going on?" cried King Henry. Princess Marigold grinned from behind the drum kit.

"This is the instrument I want to play," she said. "Aren't drums amazing!"
"They're certainly very loud," said Queen Juliet, weakly.
CRASH! went the cymbals. "Stop!" cried the king, but Marigold couldn't hear him.
Queen Juliet's head was beginning to hurt.

King Henry rushed over and gently took the drumstick from his daughter's hand.
"Your brother, Prince Teddy, plays the drums," he said. "We don't really need
another drummer in the family."

"I love it though," replied Marigold, lifting her arm to bash the biggest drum.
Somehow, the drumstick flew out of her hand and landed in the flowerpot behind her.
"Oh, dear. That keeps happening," she said. "Maybe I should learn something else?"
"Yes please!" agreed her parents.

The next morning, there was a terrible screeching noise coming from upstairs. Queen Juliet wondered if the palace cats were having a terrible fight and rushed upstairs to look. She found Marigold in Princess Lavender's bedroom.

"Marigold wanted me to teach her the violin," said Princess Lavender. Marigold grinned and made the terrible screeching sound again. "I just need a bit more practice!" she said. "It's brilliant fun though."

"I'm sure it is," sighed the queen. "Could practice wait until after two o'clock in the afternoon, please?" The queen wanted to make sure that she went out for a ride at two o'clock, so she'd be far away from that terrible din.

After a week, everyone in the palace had complained to the king. "Please, please can Marigold learn another instrument?" they begged.

The king had been wishing the same thing, so he went to see his youngest daughter. "Even though you play so nicely, we don't need another violinist," he said. "Why don't we ask Princess Buttercup to teach you to play the piano instead?"

"Yes, please," said Princess Marigold, happily. "It looks much easier."

However, the piano wasn't easy at all. There were too many keys and Marigold's fingers just wouldn't hit the right ones. "Oh, this is so silly!" she cried, jumping up and knocking the lid, so it nearly slammed shut on poor Buttercup's fingers.

"We'll find the right instrument for you," said the king. "Don't worry."
"Perhaps I could play your trumpet, Daddy?" asked Princess Marigold, picking up the king's shiny trumpet.

The king frowned. It wasn't easy to play the trumpet. He patiently showed Marigold how to purse her lips to play it. She giggled because he looked really funny.

Marigold copied her father and blew, but nothing happened. She tried again. Still nothing. Marigold tried and tried. However, no matter how hard she blew, she couldn't make any sound at all. After a while, Marigold's lips grew really sore. "I don't think the trumpet is the instrument for me," she told her father, sadly.

That night, Princess Marigold wandered around the palace gardens. Through the open palace windows, she could hear her father, with her brothers and sisters, all practicing their instruments. The music was so beautiful. They were all so talented, unlike her.

Marigold turned a corner and came across her mother who was playing a sad, slow song on her flute. It summed up Marigold's mood and she sang along, sadly. Suddenly, the queen stopped playing. "What's wrong, Marigold?" she asked.

"All of you are musical, apart from me," Marigold sighed. "All I want to do is to perform in the royal concert with my brother and sisters."
The queen hugged her. "You will be in the concert, I promise," she said. "I've just had a brilliant idea."

The next week, everyone from miles around gathered for the royal concert. As they all sat in the Grand Concert Hall, dressed in their finest clothes, rumors spread among them. Posters proclaimed that Princess Marigold was performing, but what would she play? Everybody had heard about her attempts to learn the drums, violin, piano and trumpet. So, was it any wonder that people secretly brought earplugs with them?

Finally, the curtain rose. All the royal family stood on the stage with their instruments and, at the very front, was Princess Marigold. Everyone leaned forward in their seats, whispering.

King Henry began playing his trumpet and the audience hushed. The rest of his family joined in on their instruments, playing the most beautiful tune. Marigold stood quietly at the front. Then, suddenly, she opened her mouth and started to sing.

Everyone was stunned. Marigold's voice was so sweet and beautiful. Everyone agreed it was the best royal concert, ever. At the end, the whole audience jumped to its feet, cheering and applauding. The loudest cheers of all were for Princess Marigold, the star of the show. She couldn't stop smiling. It seemed she was musical after all!

The Naughtiest Princess

One morning, Princess Clara was reading, quietly, when her sister, Violet, poked her head around the door and gave a naughty grin. "Oh, dear, Clara," she said. "It looks like you're in trouble again."

"What do you mean?" asked Clara, but Violet had already disappeared. Clara was worried. Her naughty sister was always playing nasty tricks and making everyone think it was her. Had Violet done it again?

Suddenly, the king called upstairs. "Clara!" he bellowed. "Come to the kitchen, now!" Clara hurried downstairs, wondering what trouble her sister had got her into.

In the kitchen, the queen was comforting Cook, who looked very upset. "What's the matter?" said Clara.

"Just look!" cried the king, pointing to Cook's special cake for the banquet that night. "Someone has been taking bites out of it. Cook will have to start all over again, now."
"I didn't touch it," protested Clara. "I haven't been in the kitchen all morning!"

"Really?" said the king, "how come your mother found your violin bow right beside the cake? It's yours isn't it?" He looked at Clara, sternly.
Clara groaned. "Yes," she said, weakly. She tried to explain, but her mother interrupted.

"Please, go to your room and don't come out until we say so," said the queen.
Clara mumbled and muttered under her breath as she trudged upstairs. "Why does Violet always get away with it," she said. "I wish something would happen to show Mum and Dad that it's not me being naughty, at all."

Clara was sulking in her bedroom when she heard Violet talking to someone in the hallway, outside. Suddenly, the door flew open. "Hello, Clara," said Princess Petunia. "I've come to visit. What are you doing sitting in here, all by yourself?"

Clara was very happy to see her cousin. She was just about to answer her when Violet interrupted. "Clara's been naughty again," she said, with a mischievous smile.

Princess Petunia just laughed. "Oh, dear, what did you do?" she asked. "Nothing," replied Clara. "Violet ate chunks of Cook's special cake and made everyone think it was me."

Petunia laughed even louder. "Do you know what I did when I was your age?" "What?" asked Violet, suddenly very curious. "I hid my dad's crown," giggled Petunia. Violet found this terribly funny. Clara groaned. She didn't want Petunia giving her naughty sister ideas.

Suddenly, Violet ran off. "Come back!" shouted Clara, but Violet ignored her. "She's probably hurrying off to steal my dad's crown and hide it under my bed, so everyone thinks it's me!" wailed Clara. "My naughty sister loves nothing better than getting me into trouble. Mum and Dad think I ruined Cook's cake today. They'll be furious with me if they think I've hidden Daddy's crown."

Petunia frowned. "Does Violet do this kind of thing often?" she asked. "Yes," replied Clara. "I'm always getting into trouble because of her tricks." "Don't you worry," replied Petunia, giving her a hug. "One of these days, Violet might just get a taste of her own medicine."

As it turned out, Violet didn't pinch the king's crown and Clara didn't get into any trouble. She was so happy, she did her best to show her parents what a good girl she was, by being polite and offering to help. "That's very kind of you, Clara," said the queen. "Could you go upstairs and fetch my tiara, please?"

Clara hurried upstairs, but she couldn't find the queen's tiara. It wasn't in her jewelry box or drawers, or anywhere. Someone must have taken it. Suddenly, in a blinding flash, Clara knew. It was Violet. It had to be. Violet had hidden the tiara, so Clara would get the blame. Clara searched, frantically, but the tiara was nowhere to be found.

Suddenly, Clara heard the king calling her name. "Come down, at once!" he shouted, angrily. Clara ran to the landing and couldn't believe her eyes. There were muddy footprints all up the stairs. The king and queen looked cross. "How could you, Clara?" cried the king. "Instead of helping, you went running around outside. You even left your dirty boots here."

"I didn't! I haven't had time!" cried Clara. "I went upstairs to get Mum's tiara."

The queen stood with her hands on her hips. "If you did go to look for my tiara, where is it?" she said. Clara looked embarrassed. "It's gone," she whispered, miserably. Once more, Clara was in trouble for something she hadn't done.

35

Clara looked down at the muddy boots. She had Violet to thank for this mess. Then, suddenly, she realised something. "These aren't my boots!" she cried, bringing the boots downstairs. "They're Violet's!" Just then, Petunia and Violet walked through the front door.

"Violet, did you make this mess?" asked the king.
"No," replied Violet, looking shocked. The queen picked up a boot and gasped. Tucked inside, was her tiara. "Violet, *you* took it!" she cried.

Violet was so shocked, she didn't know what to say. "I didn't, honestly," she squeaked. "I think you should clean these stairs, quickly," said the king. "Get some soapy water from the scullery, immediately."

Clara couldn't believe that Violet had been careless enough to be found out. Just then, she looked at Petunia. Her cousin smiled and winked at her. Suddenly, Clara understood. Petunia had used the muddy boots to make the footprints and she had hidden the tiara.

Petunia went to see Violet as she scrubbed the stairs. "You hid the tiara so I would get the blame," said Violet, angrily.

"Yes," replied Petuna. "I thought you should find out what it's like to have tricks played on you. It's not much fun, is it?" Violet slowly shook her head as she scrubbed the steps. "No," she replied, miserably.

Petunia took the cloth from Violet and smiled. "Go and tell your parents about the tricks you played on Clara, while I finish cleaning the stairs."

"That's really kind of you," said Violet and she hurried off to find the king, queen and Clara.

When she found them, Violet tearfully confessed all the things she had done to get Clara into trouble. "I'm sorry," she said, "I'll never do it again."

The king, queen and Clara forgave Violet. From then on, true to her word, Violet was always on her best behavior. After all, who knew what tricks Petunia had up her sleeve!

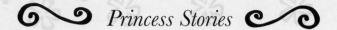
The Best Ball Gown

Princess Rose was so excited. It was the day of the Winter Ball and absolutely everyone was going. All her princess friends had come to the palace to have fun for the day and then get ready for the ball. They had such a good time, playing games, practicing their dance steps and talking excitedly about the night ahead. As they sipped strawberry milkshakes, even though she knew she shouldn't, Rose just couldn't resist putting on her new ball dress to show everyone. "Oh, it's so lovely!" cried Fenella, and everyone else agreed.

Rose smiled, proudly, as her friends gazed in wonder at the pale yellow, silk dress. It was covered in hearts and had delicate lace round the neck and sleeves. "I think it's the nicest dress I've ever had!" cried Rose, happily, twirling round to show everyone.

As Rose did, the heel on her shoe snapped and she stumbled forward, making Fenella splash her milkshake. Everyone laughed until they saw that Rose had splashed her milkshake, too and it was all over her beautiful dress! In a panic, Rose stepped back and accidentally stood on her tiara, breaking it in two.

Rose burst into tears. She had a snapped heel on her shoe, a broken tiara and a ruined dress. "Everything has gone wrong," she sobbed. "I can't go to the ball!" "Don't worry," said Fenella, wiping Rose's tears away. "We'll think of something."

39

Rose's friends all hugged her and said that, together, they would solve the problem. Suddenly, Fenella jumped up. "I've got an idea!" she cried. "Come on, we need to find the queen."

The girls followed their friend, all the way to Queen Edwina's chamber. "Your Majesty, have you got an old ball gown we can borrow?" asked Fenella. The queen smiled at her. "Of course, look in that wardrobe," she replied. "That's where I keep my old gowns."

The friends looked in the queen's wardrobe. Poppy found an elegant, blue dress. Then, Rose held up a lovely, pink one. Candy and Sally tried on pretty scarves and Fenella looked at some evening bags.

Rose thought that everything they had found was wonderful. However, the dresses were no use to her because they were all too big. "Don't worry," said Fenella. "I've got another idea."

Next, the girls went to see the king, who was trying on his best jacket for the ball. Fenella told him all about Rose's broken tiara.

The king hugged his daughter. "Don't worry," he said. "I may have something here to help you." He pulled out a chest, filled with sparkling jewelry. Everyone gasped. "They're very old royal jewels," said the king, "but maybe you'll find something useful?"

Rose selected a beautiful tiara. It would have been perfect, except that it had a big hole where the diamond should be. "It's no use at all!" she cried.

Just then, Fenella, had another idea. She led everyone to Martha, the royal dressmaker and showed her everything they'd collected from the king and queen. "Can you help us make Rose look beautiful, tonight?" she asked her. "We all want to help."

"I'll do my best," replied Martha, smiling. "I can't do anything about the tiara and that shoe may be beyond repair, but let's see what we can do about the dress." She went to the cupboard and got out a tape measure and some brightly-colored cotton. "Right, let's get to work," she said.

Martha and the girls snipped, pinned and sewed. After a while, the new ball gown began to take shape.

Everyone worked really hard, all afternoon. No one minded because it was such good fun. Finally, after a long time, the ball gown was finished.

Martha held it up and everyone gasped. The gown was pale blue with pretty lace round the sleeves and hem. Little jewels were sewn here and there and they sparkled in the sunlight. Martha had even made a pair of purple gloves with a sash to match.

Rose had been so disappointed about her yellow silk dress being spoiled, she never imagined anything would be as nice. As she slipped on the new ball gown, she realised that it was even more beautiful. Tears of happiness filled her eyes.

43

Rose hugged everyone and thanked them. Then, the girls walked back to Rose's bedroom with her. However, something occurred to Rose. She didn't have any shoes or a tiara to wear with her dress. She couldn't go barefoot and whoever heard of a princess without a tiara? Everyone had worked so hard, Rose felt that she couldn't say anything. She'd seem so ungrateful.

Suddenly, Martha came in. "I'm afraid the palace cobbler couldn't mend your shoe," she said. "However, he gave me this pair instead and they seem to be the same color as your dress."

Rose took the lovely, blue shoes and tried them on. To her amazement, they fitted and were a perfect match for her dress.

"I've also fiddled with that old tiara," said Fenella, holding it up. Rose gasped. No one could possibly see that a diamond had been missing. It was perfect!

Soon, everyone was ready. Princess Rose entered the ballroom with her friends and everyone thought they looked beautiful. "That's a very pretty ball gown you're wearing," said the queen. The orchestra played lovely music and everyone danced and danced. Rose and her friends laughed, twirled and had fun all evening.

"Are you having a good time?" asked Fenella as everyone met up to eat cupcakes. "Oh, yes," said Rose, smiling at her friends. "Everyone has been so helpful. Thanks to all of you, I've got the best ballgown, ever."

Princess Daisy and the Ordinary Day

Princess Daisy was fed up. Her palace was like a prison. Even on market day, she was only allowed to watch from the safety of her carriage. How she longed to jump out, and talk to the townsfolk, shop for dresses and taste the delicious-looking cakes and pies displayed on the stalls.

"You're so lucky!" she told her maid, Sally. "You get to go into town everyday. I'd love to be free to talk to everyone and go where I please."
"I'd love to lie in a bed as soft as yours," sighed Sally. "I'd like to eat the delicious feasts I help Cook make for you and the king and queen."

"You can!" cried Daisy, her eyes shining. "There's a feast tomorrow. Why don't we swap places? We're the same height and we look alike. If you dress as me and I dress as you, we'll fool everyone. Will you do it? Please?"
"I'd love to!" Sally grinned. "I'd love nothing more."

The next morning, Sally slipped into Daisy's room, very early. Giggling, the two girls swapped clothes. Daisy put on Sally's ordinary dress, while Sally put on Daisy's beautiful nightgown and slipped into her beautiful bed. She'd no idea it was so soft.

Outside, Daisy laughed as she skipped along the road. The birds were singing, the sun was shining, she was free! She glanced at the shopping list Cook had given Sally. It would be fun, picking the juiciest lemons, the sweetest grapes and maybe even tasting some first. However, it was a very long way to market on foot and Daisy wasn't looking forward to walking.

Finally, Daisy reached the market. She was excited to look around. The pies smelt so wonderful, she bought two. If her mother could see her wandering along eating a pie in the open air, with her fingers, she would be horrified.

Sally, meanwhile, was having a wonderful time at the palace. Daisy's bed was so comfortable, she fell fast asleep and didn't wake for hours. She opened her eyes and yawned and stretched. Normally she'd be trudging back from market. Instead, she had a bath that was almost overflowing with scented bubbles. Afterwards, she tried on Daisy's beautiful dresses and tiaras. She danced around the bedroom, imagining herself at a ball.

Suddenly, the door opened and the queen came in. Sally froze. Was she in trouble? The queen just smiled. She didn't even notice that Sally was pretending to be her daughter. "You look so pretty in that dress," she said. "You should wear it to the banquet tonight."

Back at the market, the town clock chimed mid-day and Daisy jumped. She was supposed to be back at the palace by now. Where was her shopping list? She must've dropped it. What was she supposed to get? She had no idea. In the end, Daisy just bought a bag of potatoes and a melon and hurried back. The shopping was so heavy, she felt as though her arms were dropping off.

At the palace, the cook wasn't even grateful. "Where are the chickens?" she cried. "Where are the lemons and grapes and strawberries? I can't make a feast with potatoes and a melon!"

"Um," Daisy began, tearfully.

"I'll have to go myself!" Cook said. "You can stay here and wash all the pots and pans!"

50

In another part of the palace, Sally had been trying to learn her dance steps. She wasn't doing very well. The moment she stepped onto the dance floor, everyone would guess her secret.

Sally peeped into the Banqueting Hall. The tables were neatly set. Everything looked beautiful but, instead of feeling excited, Sally feel really nervous. What would she talk about? She was going to make such a fool of herself. All that delicious food and she'd be too nervous to eat it!

"Are you excited?" said a voice, over her shoulder. Sally jumped. It was the queen again. "Tonight is your chance to impress Prince John," said the queen. "Maybe he'll ask you to dance with him?" Sally frowned. Not if he saw the way she danced!

Soon, the banquet began and Sally sat glumily at one of the tables. Meanwhile, Daisy's arms ached from carrying heavy plates of food into the banquet. She was very hungry and Cook was so cross with her, she hadn't let her eat a thing. "Whoops!" she said, as she knocked the Duke of Dandy's arm. He was furious as wine went all over his best, red jacket.

Daisy glanced at Sally. She was so lucky to be sitting there, about to be served yummy food, but she didn't look at all happy. Daisy could see that Sally didn't know which knife or fork to use. "I don't know what to do or say," Sally whispered. "Please help me!"

Suddenly, the king stood up. "Ladies and gentlemen," he announced. "Before we start dancing, Princess Daisy will play the harp."

Sally was horrified. She didn't know how to play the harp. Daisy thought quickly. There was only one thing to do. She tipped her jug of gravy all over Sally's dress. "Oh!" she cried. "Sorry!"
"Dear me," said the queen, frowning. "Quick, Daisy, go and get changed before you play.

Sally gave a sigh of relief as Daisy offered to go upstairs with her and help her change. Giggling, the girls swapped their clothes. Sally got a clean outfit for Daisy and they rushed back into the Banqueting Hall. As Daisy played her harp and Sally cleared away the plates, they both smiled. Each of them realised that they liked their lives just as they were!

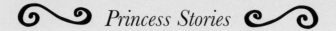

Princess Olivia's Hero

Prince Derek was very excited when he received an invitation to compete in the Prince of the Year competition on June 12th. As well as receiving a gold cup, the winner would dance the first dance at the celebration ball with Princess Olivia, the most beautiful princess in the land. Derek wished more than anything that he wasn't so thin and weak. "If only I could transform myself and win the prize," he said.

Derek decided that he was going to get fit. So, he ran up the hill to his castle, but he had to stop half-way because of a stitch in his side. He tried to do twenty press ups, but only managed five. Then, he checked his reflection and frowned. "I'm as thin as ever," he sighed. "What chance do I have of becoming Prince of the Year?"

Each day, Derek tried to get fitter. He jogged and lifted weights. By June 11th he'd even managed to do ten press-ups. However, somehow, he didn't look any different. His legs were as thin and spindly as ever and the muscles on his arm even seemed to have shrunk!

"It's useless!" cried Derek, flopping onto his bed. "I'll never be as good as the other princes. I might as well stay at home tomorrow." However, he thought about the prize and dancing with Princess Olivia. He would enter the competition. Even if he came last, he had to try.

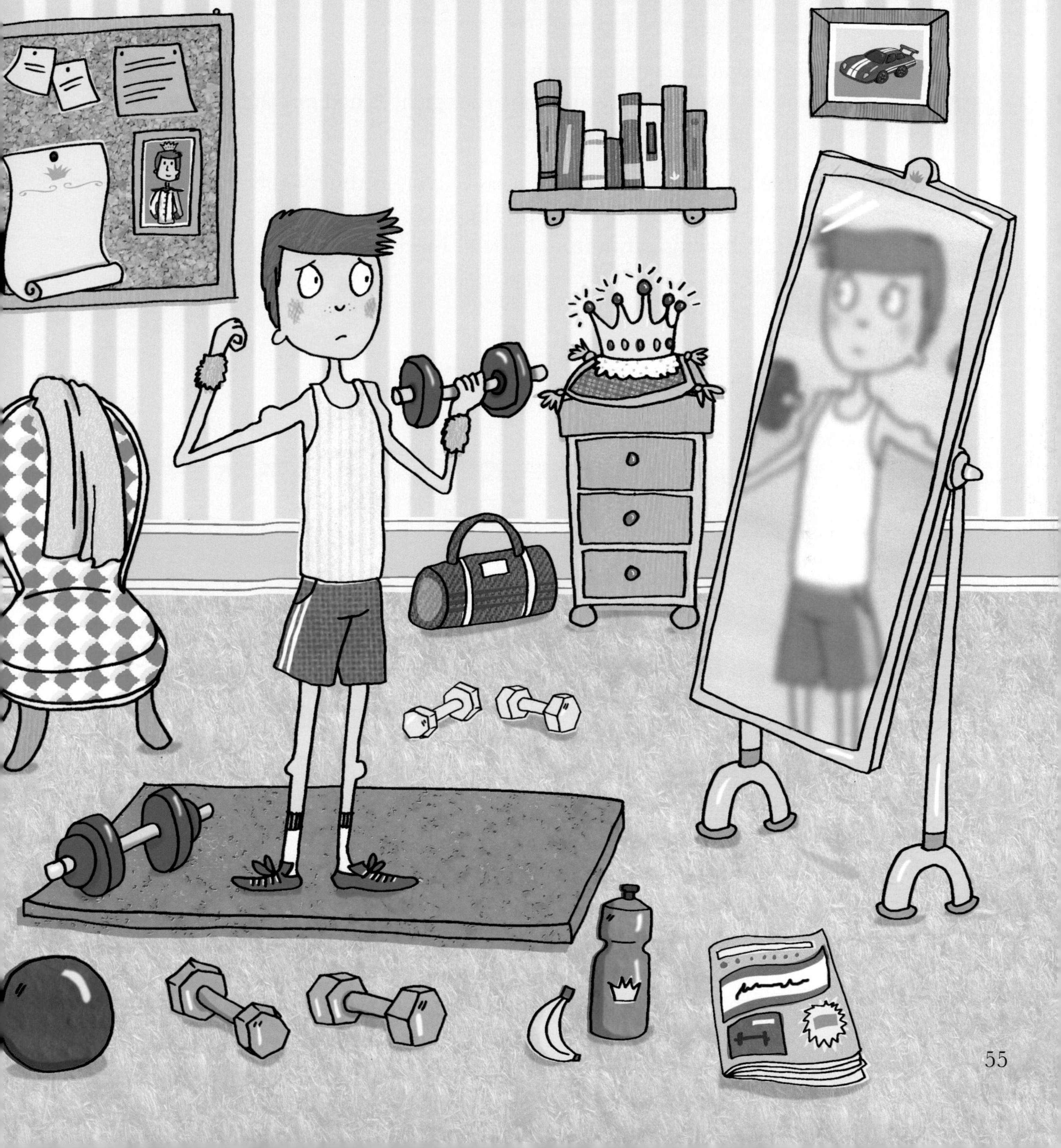

When Derek arrived at the palace grounds, he almost decided to go back home. The first event was a swimming race and the other princes had put their wetsuits on. They all looked so fit and handsome and they had such big muscles!

Derek turned to go, but then he saw Princess Olivia, in the royal box. She looked so pretty, but so sad. "No wonder she's unhappy," he said to himself. "She must be fed up of big-headed princes showing off in front of her." *The princes might be fit and handsome,* thought Derek, *but they are also loud, boring and self-important.*

In the royal box, Olivia yawned as the trumpet sounded the first challenge. There was a lot of splashing and cheering. Then, suddenly, the crowd roared with laughter. Olivia frowned. What was happening? One of the princes had stopped swimming.

"I've got cramp!" yelled Prince Derek, splashing to the side. He staggered up the bank, hopped around for a while and then stood there, dripping. Derek smiled, sheepishly, at Princess Olivia. She couldn't help but giggle. Somehow, he didn't seem like all the other princes. For one thing, he was half their size.

Derek bowed to the beautiful princess and smiled. He shivered so much however, the princess sent her maid to wrap a towel around him.

57

The princess' smile warmed Derek more than the towel. "So what if I've failed the first challenge," he told himself. "Maybe the horse riding will suit someone nimble and light, like me."

At the start of the horse race, Derek sat on his pony and sneezed. He'd forgotten that he was allergic to horses. "What's the matter with you?" sneered one of the princes, galloping past.

Poor Derek was so busy blowing his nose, he missed the beginning of the race. He cantered along behind and almost caught up, when a huge sneezing fit sent him tumbling off his horse, into a muddy puddle.

Next, was the sword fighting event. Derek felt really nervous. The swords looked really heavy. Derek could hardly pick his up. Princess Olivia cheered him on and that made him feel better. However, when he did manage to finally pick up his sword, it was so heavy, Derek toppled backwards into a pile of nettles. Everyone roared with laughter. "Oh, no," gasped Olivia, feeling very sorry for him

Everyone else was so busy laughing at Derek, they didn't see three robbers, creeping across the palace grounds. Derek saw them, but nobody could hear him shouting because they were all laughing so much. "I've got to do something," said Derek.

As Derek crept near the show tent, he heard voices inside. "Hurry up, grab the cup!" said one of the robbers. Derek peered inside and saw the robbers stealing the prizes. He had to stop them. But they looked fierce and there was no way someone puny like him could defeat them. Desperately, he looked around, but there was no one nearby.

Suddenly, Derek had an idea. The tent was held up with ropes, fixed into the ground by pegs. Carefully, Derek crept round and pulled out all the pegs. The ropes loosened and, suddenly, the tent started to collapse, trapping the robbers inside. As they shouted angrily, trying to find their way out, Derek called for the king's guard. "Got you!" he cried, triumphantly to the trapped burglars.

When everyone saw Derek beside the collapsed show tent, they thought that he'd been clumsy again. Derek quickly explained and the robbers were arrested. "Well done!" cried the king. "You saved the prizes. Three cheers for Prince Derek!"

Derek could hardly reply, he was so shy and Princess Olivia was smiling at him again. "Prince Derek is a real hero," she said. "Not only has he entertained us all, but he has been so brave. He should be crowned Prince of the Year."

The king agreed and presented Derek with the cup. He might be the clumsiest, weakest prince in the land, but Derek was also the luckiest. Princess Olivia took his arm and thought that she was the luckiest princess, too.

The Rude Princess

Princess Alice woke up cross. Her maid, Mary, knew that this was nothing unusual. Princess Alice usually woke up in a bad mood but, today, she seemed worse than ever. Mary held her breath as she tip-toed into the princess' bedroom and gently pulled her curtains. "Don't be so noisy!" cried Alice. "The sunlight is far too bright!"

"Sorry, your highness," whispered Mary. She held her breath as she opened the wardrobe door and took out a dress for her mistress to wear. "I'm not wearing that!" shouted Alice. "I want to wear my best party dress."
"You're not going to a party today, your Highness," replied Mary, as kindly as she could. "So what!" snapped Alice, "I still want to wear it!"

Just then, Prince Rupert came in. "Come on, Sis," he said. "Let's go outside and play." Alice felt really cross. "Oh, go away," she said, grumpily. "I don't want to play with you, you're boring." Prince Rupert went off in a huff and poor Mary had to spend hours getting Alice dressed and doing her hair in the most elaborate style.

When she was ready, Alice swept into the breakfast room, just as the queen was finishing her breakfast. "You're very late, darling," she said. Alice just sighed and blamed Mary. Just then, the cook placed her breakfast in front of her. "Oh, no!" she cried, pushing her plate away. "Not eggs, again!"

The queen gently tried to persuade her daughter to eat her breakfast. "Darling, you'll be hungry later if you don't eat anything," she said. "Cook prepared your eggs just how you like them. He'll be upset if you waste good food."
"Who cares!" replied Alice, sulkily.

"I do!" thundered the king. He stood up and looked cross. "I've had enough of your bad behaviour, Alice. Stop making a fuss and eat up your breakfast."
"No, I don't want to!" shouted Alice and she got up and ran away, as fast as she could, out into the palace gardens.

Alice felt like being naughty. She got mud on her party dress and it tore on some rose thorns. She knew that Mary could fix it and went back into the palace to find her.

When she got there, Alice was surprised to find the palace was empty. In the throne room, she found a note that said, *You've upset everyone, so we've all left the palace. If you are sorry and won't be rude again, raise the blue flag on the battlements.*

"I'm not doing that!" cried Alice and her voice echoed through the silent palace. Then, she smiled to herself. This was her chance to have fun. She got out all her paints and started creating wonderful, colorful pictures, not caring where the paint went.

Alice loved being able to do whatever she wanted, with no stuffy parents telling her off all the time. She danced around the ballroom, singing her favorite tunes at the top of her voice. No one could hear her, no matter how loud she sang.

Suddenly, Alice had the most wonderful idea. Giggling, she ran up to her mother's bedroom and pulled out her best dress, to try on over her own. Then, she put on her mother's tiara, necklace and rings. After that, Alice bounced on her parents' lovely, springy bed. It was great fun for a while, but soon, Alice found the dresses too hot and wanted to take them off.

"Mary!" she shouted. "Help me take off these dresses. However, Mary had gone off with the others. So, Alice had to wriggle out of the dresses on her own.

Alice looked at her ruined party dress, lying, crumpled on the bed. *I always loved that dress,* she thought, sadly. *If I had listened to Mary, this morning, it wouldn't have got spoiled.* Alice went back to her own room and put on the dress that Mary had left out for her.

Suddenly, being able to do exactly what she liked didn't feel so good. Alice's tummy was rumbling with hunger. She wished she hadn't been so mean about Cook's breakfast. Alice really missed Prince Rupert, too. If she hadn't been rude to him, they could be playing together, right now.

Alice realised that she missed everyone. So, she tidied up all the mess she had made and climbed the narrow, winding stairs up to the battlements. Alice raised the blue flag.

Then, she waited and waited, peering into the distance. Had her parents given up looking for the flag, after all this time? Could they even see it from where they'd gone? How she missed everyone. Alice started to feel very alone.

Suddenly, she saw something glinting in the sun, in the distance. The royal carriage was driving back towards the palace. Alice cheered and waved, wildly. "Hooray!" she cried. They were coming back.

Alice rushed out to greet the royal carriage. As her mother and father and Prince Rupert climbed out, she hugged and kissed them all. She even hugged Cook and Mary, who giggled and looked embarrassed. "I'm so sorry!" Alice cried. "No wonder you left me. I was really horrible to everyone. I won't be mean any more, I promise."

So, from that day on, Alice was polite to everyone. She ate up all her meals, without complaint and played, happily, with Prince Rupert. After all, she knew it was really lonely being in a castle on her own and besides, no one liked a rude princess.

Fashionable Harriet

Princess Harriet laughed to herself as she rode her bike down the steep path. She bumped over stones and shrieked, as mud splattered everywhere. It was brilliant fun. The dirtier she got, the funnier it was. Then, Harriet turned a corner and skidded to a halt, frowning.

Below her, the palace grounds were a hive of activity. A marquee had been put up and servants were carrying out chairs, tables and armfuls of flowers. The garden party for the Spring Festival was taking place that afternoon. Harriet would be expected to wear a silly dress and walk around in flimsy shoes that couldn't even kick a football. As if that wasn't bad enough, tonight she would have to go to the boring Spring Ball.

Harriet wished that she was a boy. Then, she wouldn't have to wear dresses, or go to boring royal events. She could climb trees and have fun, all day long.

Suddenly, her maid, Lucy, came running along the path. "Oh, there you are, Your Highness," she said. "Your mother sent me. It's time to get ready for the garden party."

Lucy laughed as she looked at Harriet's wild hair, mud-splattered face and clothes. Harriet grinned back. "Wouldn't it be fun to go to the garden party like this?" she said. "That would give everyone something interesting to talk about."

Harriet sighed and started cycling back to the palace. *Whoosh*, she went through a stream. "Whee!" she cried, as water sploshed everywhere. "What fun!"

Queen Margaret was horrified when she saw her daughter. "Princess Bella's arriving any minute!" she cried. "If she writes a bad report about the Spring Festival in her column in *Royal Events*, our reputation will be totally ruined. She mustn't see you looking like this. Go and have a bath, quick!"

Harriet sighed and did as she was told, but refused to have smelly bubbles in the water. Afterwards, the queen held up two pretty, new dresses. "Just pick one, please," she said. "I don't like them," replied Harriet. "I want to wear my jeans until the party starts."

The queen promised to buy Harriet a new bike. She threatened to take away her football kit, but Harriet wouldn't budge. She would only put on a skirt when the garden party began, but not a minute before.

Princess Bella arrived twenty minutes later, wearing an elegant, pink dress, with matching jewelry and a case full of dresses to change into every half-hour.

"Oh, doesn't Bella look beautiful?" said Queen Margaret, turning to Harriet in her t-shirt and jeans. She shuddered in horror. They were covered in rips and tears. "Yes," replied Harriet, politely. "Do you want to ride my bike Bella?" "Oh, no!" said Bella, horrified. "I'll get my dress dirty. I'll just sit and read my magazine."

Bella held up *Royal Events*, which, as far as Harriet could see, was a magazine completely filled with dresses. There was no sport, or bikes, or anything interesting. So, she left Bella reading, while she went off to have fun while she could.

After lunch, the queen sent servants to search for Harriet. Finally, Lucy found her covered in oil, fixing the chain on her bike. "Oh, Your Highness. Come and have your bath, now, please," she begged. Harriet sighed. "Not another bath. How boring!"

Afterwards, Lucy brought out a frilly, purple ball dress covered in bows and sequins. "I can't wear that!"cried Harriet. "I'll look like a girl!"
However, the queen had taken away Harriet's mucky jeans, locked her wardrobe door and hidden the key. Even Harriet wouldn't go to the garden party naked. She had no choice but to wear the ball dress.

Reluctantly, Harriet put on the dress. Instead of tights and dainty high-heeled shoes however, she chose red, orange and blue leggings and her pink boots. Smiling at her reflection, she put gel in her and piled it up high. Harriet might have to wear a dress, but she was still going to liven up the garden party.

Queen Margaret nearly fainted when Harriet walked out onto the lawn. She ran to her daughter, hoping to send her back inside, before Bella saw. However, it was too late. Bella had already seen Harriet.

The queen froze. Bella would write terrible things about Harriet's awful outfit. Their reputation would be ruined. Everyone turned and stared at Harriet. Then they looked at Bella. What would she say? Suddenly, Bella spoke. "I love your outfit," she cried. "You look so cool."

Everyone at the garden party breathed a sigh of relief and nodded their heads in agreement. Harriet walked among the guests and everybody admired her cool, new look. It seemed the garden party was a big hit and it was all thanks to her.

That night, everyone was excited as they got ready for the ball. Everyone, except Queen Margaret. "Now, dear, you can't possibly wear your leggings and boots to the ball," she told Harriet. "Please put on your pretty, high heels and wash that ghastly gel out of your hair. Lucy will put it in a bun."

Harriet, however, refused to change. "No, mother," she said. "I'll wear a dress to make you happy, but everything else stays as it is."

The queen pleaded with Harriet. She suggested tights or paler leggings and different shoes, but Harriet liked her new look. It was fun and anyway, she couldn't dance in high heels. Boots and leggings were perfect.

The queen was convinced everyone would laugh at Harriet at the ball. She was dreading going in there. As she led Harriet into the ballroom, the queen couldn't believe her eyes. All the princesses had spiky hair and were wearing bright leggings and boots, just like Harriet.

The queen burst out laughing. Who would have thought it? Her daughter was a fashion icon. *Royal Events* would be full of the new fashion at the Spring Festival thanks to her wonderful, trend-setting daughter. She smiled at Harriet. Never again would she tell her what to wear!

Georgia and the Dragon

Princess Georgia swung by her legs, from her favorite tree in the castle gardens. Everything looked very strange and not just because she was upside-down. It was because all the other trees in the garden had been chopped down for firewood.

Suddenly, Georgia froze in horror. The woodcutter was walking towards her tree with his axe. "No!" she cried and, with a double somersault, she threw herself from the tree to block his path. "Don't cut down this tree."

The surprised woodcutter explained that he was simply carrying out the king's orders. "No!" Georgia wailed, running into the palace. "No!" she wailed, racing up the stairs, two at a time and nearly bumping into her mother. "Georgia, for once, please behave like a Princess," said the Queen. "What's the matter?"

Georgia begged her mother to stop the woodcutter chopping down the last tree, but the queen calmly explained that it was needed for firewood. It had been such a cold winter, every other tree for miles, including the local woods, had been chopped down and the town's people were shivering and hungry.

"We can get wood from the Dark Forest," cried Georgia. As she said this, the servants gasped and the queen went pale. "No, Georgia, we can't," she whispered. "Remember the dragon?"

Georgia did remember the dragon. There were lots of stories about how fierce he was. However, no one had ever actually seen him. "So, a silly dragon lives there," said Georgia. "People say he's fierce and rather fond of eating people, but it's time someone stood up to him."

Despite Georgia's protests, the last tree was chopped down and burnt and then, there were no more fires. A cold wind blew and snow began to fall. The castle grew icier and everyone felt terribly cold. "I'm freezing," shivered Georgia. "Someone *must* go and ask the dragon for help." However, everyone was too wrapped up with scarves and hats over their ears to hear her.

So, Georgia jumped onto Smudge, her horse. "Well, I'll just have to go myself," she said and she galloped off, out of the palace, before anyone noticed.

As Georgia galloped along, all she could think about was how she longed to be warm. However, as the Dark Forest loomed closer, she Georgia to think about the dragon. Was he very scary? Did he really eat people? Even little girls?

When they came to the forest, Smudge was too scared to enter, so Georgia tip-toed in on her own. Hardly any sunlight shone through the trees and everywhere was still and silent. As Georgia walked on through the gloom, she told herself that her trembling legs shook from cold, not fear.

At last, she reached a cave with scorch marks on the walls. It had to be where the dragon lived. "I am not scared," Georgia told herself as she crept closer.

Suddenly, a twig snapped, loudly, under her feet. It made her jump. "Who goes there?" boomed an angry voice. Georgia peered into the darkness. All she could see were two, big, round, golden eyes staring back at her. She had come face-to-face with the dragon.

Georgia wanted to turn and run, but instead she whispered, "Hello."
"What are you doing in my cave?" boomed the dragon. Georgia gulped.
"I've come to see you," she replied, shaking.

"Come to see me?" replied the dragon. "Why?" he boomed. Suddenly, smoke curled from his nostrils. No doubt the dragon was wondering whether to fatten her up before eating her.

Georgia explained that the only trees left were the ones in the Dark Forest. "Everyone's freezing because we have no firewood. They are too scared to come here to get some, because you'll eat them!"

The dragon came closer and Georgia felt afraid. She'd reminded him how he liked eating humans. Now he was going to eat her!

However, instead of eating Georgia, the dragon began to cry and she realised that he was only a baby. "I'm so lonely," he sobbed. "I don't want to eat people. I just want someone to play with. Will you play with me?"

Georgia felt really sorry for the dragon. She named him Gilbert and suggested they play hide–and–seek. It was very easy to find Gilbert, because whenever Georgia came near him, he got so excited that he breathed out huge flames. They were so lovely and warm, they made Georgia think of her cold family and she felt guilty.

"Can I collect some firewood to take home?" she asked.
"Yes," replied Gilbert. "I have one condition, though," and he bent down to whisper into Georgia's ear.

83

Georgia and Gilbert hurriedly collected a pile of firewood. Then, Georgia climbed onto Gilbert's back and they flew to her castle, with Smudge trotting, happily, behind.

The king couldn't believe his eyes when he saw his precious daughter, flying home on the fiercest dragon in the kingdom. Everyone ran to hide. They dived into cupboards, under tables and chairs, trembling with fear. "Don't be afraid!" cried Georgia. "Look, we've brought firewood!"

Everyone came out of their hiding places to watch in wonder, as Georgia laid a huge fire. Then, with one blow of his fiery breath, Gilbert set it alight. As they saw smoke coming out of the castle chimneys, villagers came running to get warm, too.

The king held a big feast to celebrate. There was laughter, games and dancing. Then, the king proposed a toast to Gilbert, for offering them his wood and not expecting anything in return. "Actually, there is one condition," said Georgia. Everyone looked fearful. The king looked especially nervous. "Does he want our gold and jewels?" he asked.

"No," replied Georgia, hugging Gilbert. She explained that Gilbert was lonely and wanted to live in the castle with everyone. "Can he stay, please, Daddy," pleaded Georgia. Gilbert held his breath. "Of course he can!" replied the king. "Not only will we have a new friend, but our very own pet fire-lighter!"

Gilbert danced for joy and everyone cheered. Georgia's cheers were the loudest of all. Not only was there going to be plenty of firewood to keep everyone warm, now she had her very own dragon!

Princess Freya and the Magical Horse

Princess Freya loved horses. More than anything in the world, she wanted one of her own. One morning, when the king was leading a royal procession through the town, Freya noticed a horse in the market place. He was the most beautiful thing Freya had ever seen.

The horse was white, with a silvery-colored mane and tail. He stood so tall, elegant and proud. Freya shouted, "Stop!" She dashed from the royal coach and ran over to the horse, who whinnied and nuzzled her hand. "Oh, Daddy, can I have him, please, can I?" pleaded Freya.

By now, the whole market had stopped to look. The king came over and spoke to the merchant who owned the horse. After talking for a long time, the king shook the man's hand and walked over to Freya. "The horse is yours," he said. "His name is Firefly and I had to pay a lot of money for him. This merchant says there is no other horse like him in the world. He is very special."

Freya was so excited, she hardly heard her father's words. "Oh, thank you, Daddy," she said, climbing onto Firefly. "Go, Firefly, go!" she cried. Firefly trotted, cantered and then, galloped, as fast as the wind, all the way back to the royal palace.

Each morning, from then on, Freya got up early to ride Firefly. It was a magical time, when the fields glistened with dew. As they cantered along, Firefly moved so smoothly, Freya felt as if she was floating. She did wonder why the merchant had said Firefly was so special. However, it didn't really matter. Freya was just glad to have such a beautiful horse to ride.

Sometimes, Freya's brother, Prince Jacob, rode with her on his horse, Midnight, and they ventured far across the fields. Freya loved showing Jacob how wonderful Firefly was as he effortlessly leapt over fallen trees and streams.

One day, Freya galloped ahead of Jacob. She rode into the forest, eager to find more fallen trees to jump. "Freya, wait!" yelled Jacob from behind.

Freya stopped Firefly and peered around. The forest looked dark and gloomy. Trees crowded out the sun. Then, as Jacob cantered up, Freya gasped. In the dim gloom, she could see yellow, menacing eyes glinting. Firefly whinnied and stamped his feet. "Wolves," whispered Jacob. "Come on, let's get out of here, quick. The forest is filled with wolves," Jacob told Freya. "You must never go in there alone."

Freya just thought the wolves were silly. The first chance she got, she rode back to the forest. However, at the edge of the trees, Firefly whinnied and stopped. He could sense danger. "Come on, boy," said Freya, leaping off him. "Don't worry about the wolves. If you don't harm them, they won't hurt you."

Suddenly, Freya heard a whining sound. By the path was a litter of wolf puppies, playing in the sunlight. Then, she heard a terrible, menacing, growl. Freya turned round, slowly, to see an adult wolf, with fierce eyes, looking at her.

Freya was petrified. She was standing between a wolf mother and her puppies, the most dangerous place to be. Any moment, the wolf mother might attack to protect her young family.

Freya leapt onto Firefly's back. Then, suddenly, another wolf appeared in front, snapping and snarling. They were trapped! A trickle of fear ran down Freya's spine as Firefly reared up, then turned and galloped in another direction. Freya could hear the howls of other wolves getting closer. It seemed that the whole pack was after them.

Suddenly, a wolf appeared, snapping at Firefly's heels. Freya closed her eyes. Why had she put herself and Firefly in such danger? Surely, there was no way that they could escape now?

Suddenly, Freya felt a movement beneath her, as though she was floating through the air. She opened her eyes to see that Firefly had sprouted wings. They were flying! Far below them, she could see the wolves, still growling, angrily, because the horse and its rider had escaped.

When Freya had recovered from the shock, she clung to Firefly's mane, laughing with delight as they passed over farms and villages, hills, woods and fields. It was amazing, just like a dream!

92

Suddenly, the castle turrets came into view. "We're nearly home!"cried Freya. Firefly soared gently over the battlements, going slower and slower, until his hooves landed, gently, on the courtyard cobbles.

Freya leant forward and stroked her beautiful horse's neck. "Thank you, oh, thank you, Firefly," she whispered, her heart pounding, wildly. "You saved my life. That merchant was right, you are special, you're magic!" As Firefly whinnied softly and shook his mane, Freya knew he would always look after her and make sure she was safe. Truly, she was the luckiest princess in the world to have her own magic horse!

The Princesses and the Mermaid

Princess Sophie stepped out of the coach, in front of the old castle and her heart sank. This was going to be her new home. Her sister, Princess Ava, wouldn't get out of the coach at all. Sophie exchanged a worried glance with her mother, Queen Julia. They both thought the castle looked small and not at all inviting.

"Now girls, I know this isn't going to be nearly as grand as the palace that you're used to," said the queen. "However, we simply can't afford such elegance any more. We all have to adapt and make the best of it. I'm sure you'll soon come to love your new home as much as your old one."

Sophie was sure she wouldn't. For a start, none of her friends lived nearby and there were no tennis courts, or swimming pool to play in. Ava and Sophie had tiny bedrooms, right next door to one another. They were far too small for a sleepover with friends. The only advantage was that the walls were so old and thin, they could lie on their beds and tap messages to each other about how unhappy they were.

"There's nothing to do here," moaned Ava, as they went downstairs. "I'm bored and I've only been here five minutes."
"Why don't you explore the castle?" said the queen. "Make it into a game. You could play hide-and-seek."

"Hide-and-seek won't last long," said Sophie. "This place is so small, we'll soon run out of places to hide."
Ava shrugged. What else was there to do? "You hide and I'll find you," she told her sister. "Go on."

So, Sophie ran off down the hall. Soon, she found herself in the kitchen, where Cook was moaning about the state of the ovens. "Pretend you haven't seen me," said Sophie, grinning. She opened a door that she thought led outside. However, it didn't. It led into a narrow, dark corridor. She followed it, then turned into another corridor, then another. There were so many passageways, it was like a rabbit warren. *Ava will never find me down here*, thought Sophie, grinning.

Sophie waited and waited. She was right. Ava didn't find her. Maybe she'd given up? Sophie's tummy rumbled. It had been a long journey and she was hungry. She hoped that Cook had managed to get the ovens to work.

Sophie trudged back to where she thought the kitchen was, but she couldn't find it. In fact, she couldn't find anything she recognised. Sophie started to worry. Which way had she come? Why hadn't she noticed where she was going? Would she ever find her way back?

After she'd walked for ten more minutes, Sophie only knew one thing for sure that she was well and truly lost.

Suddenly, Sophie saw daylight ahead. She ran towards it and stepped through a door that led outside. There, she saw a big lake with beautiful, crystal clear water. In the lake, brightly-colored fish darted about under the surface. Frogs croaked and insects fluttered and swooped in the air. *Wow*, thought Sophie. *This is amazing!*

Suddenly, Sophie heard a yell. "Help!" cried a voice. "Somebody, help me, please!"

Sophie saw a girl, lying on a rock, by the side of the lake. She was tugging her hair, which seemed to be caught in some fishing line. "I'm coming!" cried Sophie, running towards the girl. When she reached her, Sophie started trying to untangle the girl's beautiful hair, but it was very difficult.

"Please hurry!" cried the girl. "If I'm out of the water much longer, I will die." Sophie stared at her, surprised. Suddenly, there was a splash and Sophie saw that, instead of legs, the girl had a beautiful, shimmery, tail. She was a mermaid!

"Please, be quick!" cried the mermaid, whose name was Miranda. Sophie tugged and tugged, but it was useless. "I need to get help," she said. "I'll be quick, I promise."

Sophie had never run so fast. "Please let me find the way back," she begged, as she followed one passageway after another. Miraculously, she found the door into the kitchen and burst through it. "That's where you are!" cried Ava, who had been searching for her sister. "I've been looking everywhere for you."

"Quick, come with me," gasped Sophie. "Hurry." She explained about Miranda as she led Ava along the passagway that led to the lake. When they got there, Miranda was so grateful to see them. The sisters worked together to untangle the mermaid's hair and soon managed to free Miranda.

"Thank you so much," said Miranda, slipping into the water. "What wonderful friends you are, to have saved me. I shall come and play with you every day and tomorrow, I'll bring a special surprise." Sophie and Ava couldn't wait.

Early the next day, they hurried back to the lake and were delighted to see Miranda riding towards them, on a beautiful dolphin.

"Come and ride, too!" she cried. So, Sophie and Ava did. They laughed and shrieked, having fantastic fun. Now that they had met Miranda, Sophie and Ava both knew that they had moved into the most exciting home in the world!

The Great Treasure Hunt

Princess Scarlett shivered as she ran down the dingy stairs of the palace. It made her sad to see her home in such a state. She hardly recognised it these days.

The palace crops had failed and for months the king and queen had been running out of money. One by one, the servants had left the palace. Fires had been left unlit and rooms closed up. Bit by bit, the palace was falling into decay.

Scarlett's stomach rumbled as she joined the king and queen in front of the only fire. Maria, their last servant, came in with the lunch tray and suddenly, Maria felt excited. When she saw that there were only dry crackers and water, her heart sank.
"I'm afraid this is the last food in the palace," said Maria. "There's nothing left in the pantry."

"What are we going to do?" wailed the queen. If only we could find the palace treasure!" The king shook his head, sadly. It was true that there was a story about palace treasure, but he'd lived here all his life and never found it.

Hungry as she was, Scarlett could hardly eat. She looked at her brother, Prince Alfred, and signalled to him to follow her. "We have to do something," she said, as they shivered in the hall. "We must search the palace to see if any coins, or jewels, have been dropped anywhere."

"A few coins aren't going to save us," said Alfred.

Scarlett knew this was true, but she had to try. Otherwise, what were they going to do?

103

The prince and princess made their way to the throne room. "Let's start in here," suggested Scarlett. "Maybe the odd jewel or two might have dropped out of the royal crowns?"

Scarlett and Alfred searched high and low, but all they could find were three coins down the back of one of the thrones. "It's better than nothing," said Scarlett, smiling at Alfred. "At least we will be able to buy potatoes for dinner tonight."

Encouraged by this small find, they continued to search all the rooms in the palace, but there were no more coins anywhere. The nearest they came to treasure was a toy necklace that had belonged to one of Scarlett's dolls. "It is useless," said Alfred.

Suddenly, Scarlett had an idea. "I know," she said. "Let's go and look in the palace library. There must be something about the treasure in the royal history books. Perhaps we will find some clues."

Alfred followed Scarlett to the library. The walls were lined with all sorts of books. It would take days to search them all. "The sooner we start, the sooner we'll finish," said Scarlett. "I have a good feeling about this. Come on."

So, they started flicking their way through the books. On one of the bookcases, on the top shelf, was an ancient-looking book named, *Royal Mystery Histories*. It was covered in dust and hadn't been opened in a very long time. "This looks interesting," said Alfred and he opened the old book. As he did, a ragged piece of paper fluttered all the way down to the floor. Scarlett picked it up and read it: *Find a lion, then a rose, press it once, but mind your toes!*

"What does it mean?" asked Alfred. "We don't even have cats in the palace any more, let alone lions. Maybe it's just a silly poem?"

Scarlett frowned. Surely, it couldn't be just a poem. Wouldn't it be wonderful if it was some kind of secret message?

Suddenly, Alfred gasped. "Look!" he cried, pointing to the top of a mantelpiece on the far side of the library. There was a lion's head carved into it and below were some roses. Excitedly, Alfred pressed each one in turn. There was a sudden clunking sound and the whole fireplace slowly revolved, revealing a hidden passageway. Scarlett and Alfred crept inside. "Wow!" cried Alfred, shining his torch down the passageway. Suddenly however, the torch light dimmed, then went out. They were in complete darkness.

"Come on!" said Scarlett. "Let's keep going." Slowly, she felt her way along the stone wall until she found the outline of a door. Together, they pushed it hard and, slowly, it began to open.

"Where are we?" asked Alfred, stumbling around on the rocky floor. His torch flickered a bit and then went off again. Scarlett sank to her knees and felt around in the blackness. There was a large, hard box and something pointy, covered in funny little lumps. Then there was a strange chinking sound as Scarlett fell back on a pile of cold, round shapes.

In a panic, Alfred reached for the torch. He gave it a good shake. "Work, stupid torch," he said. Suddenly, the pale torch beam flickered back into life. "Wow!" cried Alfred.

Scarlett gasped as the torch beam lit up a huge pile of jewels and coins. There was gold, diamonds and rubies as,well as crowns, tiaras and necklaces. They'd found the lost treasure!

"We've got to tell Mum and Dad," said Alfred and he stumbled back down the passageway. When he tried to push the stone door, it would not budge. "How do we get out?" he cried. "What if we are stuck in here, forever? Maybe that's why no-one ever found the treasure."

"Don't be silly," replied Scarlett, holding the torch up to the door. In the stonework was a rose. She pressed it and they swung slowly round until they were back in the library. "Mum, Dad!" yelled Alfred, running ahead. "We've found the palace treasure!"

"Alfred, this is no time for jokes," said the queen, crossly, as he almost collided with her. However, Alfred was holding up the biggest ruby the queen had ever seen in her life.

"Show me where the treasure is!" she cried, her eyes shining.

The king and queen couldn't believe their eyes when they saw the pile of treasure. "We're no longer poor!" cried the king, grabbing the queen and twirling her around. "Hooray, hooray! We're rich again, today!"

Fires were lit, rooms were opened up and, best of all, there was lots of food. The servants rushed around, polishing, sweeping and cleaning. Soon the palace was returned to its former warmth and glory.

To celebrate, the king and queen held a special banquet, to which they invited all their friends and relations. The guests of honor, toasted by everyone, were Scarlett and Alfred. After all, they and their great treasure hunt had saved the day!

Princess Charlotte's Perfect Present

It was Princess Charlotte's birthday. She'd been looking forward to it for weeks and now that it had come, she was bubbling over with excitement. She danced into the hall as the doorbell chimed. Was that her special present from her parents being delivered?

Her maid, Mary, opened the door, but Charlotte stared, horrified, as the terrible princes, Rupert and Damien walked in. "Surprise!" called the queen, smiling at her daughter. "We know you said you didn't want a big party," beamed the king, "but we thought you deserved some guests."

"Thank you," said Charlotte, weakly. How could her parents possibly imagine she'd want those twins at her birthday? When her father had told her this morning there would be surprises, she thought he'd meant good ones, not the kind that gave you nightmares. She hadn't got over the last time the twins had visited, neither had her favorite dolls. Three of them were still headless and one was missing an arm!

"You spend so much time on your own," said the queen, "and the twins are the only royal children of your age that live nearby. Come and have fun with them."

As Charlotte reluctantly joined the princes, Hannah, Mary's daughter, watched from behind a pillar. She'd love to play with Charlotte, but she was only a servant's daughter. However, Hannah didn't trust those naughty princes one little bit. She decided that she would have to keep an eye on them for poor Charlotte's sake.

111

Meanwhile, Charlotte was trying her best with Rupert and Damien. "You have a drink, I'll be back in a minute," said Charlotte and she dashed upstairs to hide all her new presents in her bedroom.

By the time Charlotte got back downstairs, the twins had spilt their drinks over the carpet and found her birthday chocolates. "Yummy, these are lovely," grinned Damien, wiping his chocolatey fingers on the curtains.
"Come on, let's go up to your bedroom and play," said Rupert, stuffing two chocolates in his mouth at once.

"No!" cried Charlotte, but the twins barged past, ignoring her. She hoped they wouldn't find her bedroom but they remembered it from their last visit. Within minutes they were jumping up and down on her bed.

Mary could see that Charlotte was struggling to control the twins. She had to do something. "The party meal is ready, Your Majesty," she announced, hurriedly. "Lovely!" cried Charlotte. Finally she'd get the twins out of her bedroom. Just then, the king came upstairs. "Don't you want to see your special present?" the king asked, pointing outside. Charlotte gasped. Through the window, she could see what looked like a miniature castle. She dashed down the stairs and out into the garden. The twins pointed and laughed. "How silly," they said."

Outside, Charlotte was lost for words. She stood, staring at the beautiful, pink, play castle. It had turrets, pillars and battlements. It was wonderful. "Go inside!" said the queen, opening the door.

Charlotte tip-toed inside and it was amazing. There was a pretty pink carpet and a cosy settee and two arm chairs. There were pictures on the walls and fairy lights hung around the walls. "It's beautiful, thank you," gasped Charlotte, picking up a cushion and hugging it to her. Outside, Hannah watched from behind a tree and smiled. She'd sewn that cushion. She was so proud to be part of making such a wonderful present.

"What a girly present!" cried Damien and Rupert, barging in behind Charlotte. Before she could stop them, Damien was jumping on the settee and Rupert was yelling and throwing cushions. Then, they had a cushion fight. Crash! A pretty little vase smashed to the floor. Thump! A cushion hit Charlotte on the nose.

Charlotte called for her father who came running. He bent down and peered through the door. He couldn't believe his eyes. "Out!" he thundered at the naughty princes.

The twins stopped and stared at him. No-one had ever spoken to them like that before. "Come along now," called the queen, quickly through the window. "It's time to have the party meal."

115

At the table, the twins were even more badly behaved. They poked their fingers in the birthday cake and knocked the sandwiches onto the floor. It was a relief when all the food was finished and, finally, they went home, or so everyone thought. Hannah watched as, at last, Charlotte was able to play with her beautiful castle for five minutes before bedtime. "I love my play castle," Charlotte told her mother, as she tucked her in. "It's the best ever!"
"I'm so pleased," said her mother. The queen wished her daughter had someone to share it with though.

Charlotte was too excited to sleep so, she got out of bed and gazed out of the window. Suddenly, she froze. There was a light on in her new play castle. Someone was inside. What's more, there were strange shadows in the garden.

Charlotte crept downstairs and hurried across the garden. Suddenly, something grabbed her. "Aaargh!" she screamed. Damien and Rupert jumped out from the shadows. "Got you!" they laughed.

Charlotte yanked her arm free and ran away. Suddenly, a voice whispered from the bushes. "Follow me," it said. It was Hannah and she led Charlotte down a hidden path into the play castle. "I'm sorry for playing in here, earlier," Hannah said. "I just love your castle. I couldn't resist having a look inside."
"That's okay," said Charlotte. Then, suddenly, she heard a sound. It was Rupert and Damien. "Hide!" she whispered, switching off the light.

Both girls put blankets over their heads and waited until Damien and Rupert came inside. "Whooooo!" wailed Charlotte and Hannah, pretending to be ghosts. "Arrgh!" cried the twins who were so terrified, they ran away as fast as they could!

Charlotte and Hannah laughed until they cried. "Well," gasped Charlotte. "I don't think they'll be back any time soon."

"No," said Hannah, looking around the play palace. "How I wish this was mine," she said. "I'd have parties and play games, you're so lucky."

"Yes, I know," replied Charlotte. "However, I've got no one to play with. There's no one my age except those awful twins." Suddenly, Charlotte had an idea. "Why don't we play together? You can be my friend." Hannah looked sad. She was thinking that the king and queen would never allow a servant's daughter to play with a princess.

Just then, they heard the king and queen's voices. They had been woken by all the commotion. "What's going on?" they said. "Who's in there?"

The two girls came out looking very sheepish. Charlotte explained everything. "Can I play with Hannah sometimes?" she begged. "Please? She isn't royal, but she's so lovely and such fun."

"Of course!" said her mother, hugging her. "All we want is for you to be happy. You can play with her all the time, but not tonight. Now, it's time for bed."

Charlotte was thrilled. Hannah couldn't believe her ears. "That's wonderful!" she cried. Charlotte thought so, too. She knew she'd never been happier. She had a new friend and the most amazing play castle. It had been the best birthday ever!

Princess Lola and the Crown

Princess Lola was very excited. Her two best friends, Princess Emelia and Princess Thea had come for a sleepover. "Look at me," giggled Emelia, as she tried on Lola's new ball gown, with her spotty boots!
"No, look at me!" cried Thea, as she pinned her hair up so it looked like a pineapple.
"I have the maddest friends," laughed Lola. "Come on, let's dance."

The princesses twirled round and round Lola's bedroom until, finally, it was time for bed. They were too excited to sleep. Instead, they told each other ghost stories. Then, because they were so scared, the girls told silly jokes. None of their jokes were very good, but somehow, the more awful they were, the more they laughed. Soon, they were in fits of giggles.

Suddenly, Lola's maid peered in the doorway. "I've been sent to tell you to be quiet," she said, but she couldn't help giggling, too.

"I can't sleep," sighed Emelia, after the maid had gone. "All that laughing's made me hungry."
"Let's have a midnight feast!" cried Lola. "Cook made the yummiest cookies today."

So, the girls put on their dressing gowns and, trying not to laugh, crept along the dark palace corridors, towards the kitchen.

121

As they tip-toed past one door, there was a loud snoring sound. "That's my dad!" giggled Lola. Emelia ran ahead. "Pleased to meet you," she said, shaking the hand of a suit of armor. It rattled so noisily, it made Thea jump. "Ssh," said Lola. "You'll wake everyone up."

To get to the kitchen, the girls had to go through the throne room. As Lola led the way, the others gasped to see the crown jewels glinting in the moonlight. "Can we touch them?" asked Emelia.

Lola was sure her father would be really cross if he knew what they were doing, but she just couldn't resist showing the jewels to her friends, and trying them on, too. She loved wearing her mother's long, elegant robe and her beautiful, sparkling jewelry.

Lola felt so grown up. Excitedly, she took off one set of jewels, then put on a beautiful sapphire choker and ear-rings. Emelia, meanwhile, couldn't resist picking up the royal sceptre and waving it to an imaginary crowd.

Thea chose to try on a sapphire necklace and a sparkly tiara. "I'd wear this with a midnight blue, velvet gown," she said, twirling around, "and everyone who saw me, would fall in love with me."

Thea looked at the king's crown and then looked at Lola. Put it on, Lola, go on, I dare you!" Lola hesitated. There was nothing more precious than the king's crown. Gently, she picked it up. Her father would be really cross if he saw her now.

Carefully, Lola put the crown on her head. "Oh, it's so heavy," she gasped. "I can hardly turn my head. How does my father manage? If I had to wear it all day, I'd be so grumpy!"
"Try walking," Emelia urged her.

So, Lola walked slowly, up and down. She could feel the crown slipping further and further down her head. Then, she sat down, heavily. The crown slipped even more, right over her nose. "Help!" cried Lola, trying in vain to pull off the crown. "If my father discovers I've been trying on his precious crown, he'll be furious." Emelia and Thea rushed to help pull it off. But they couldn't move the crown. It was stuck!

"Try harder," pleaded Lola. She bent forwards and Emelia and Thea tugged at the crown, with all their might, while Lola pushed herself backwards. Suddenly, the crown came free and, with no-one pulling her forwards any more, Lola went flying backwards. She knocked against the plinth and sent the crown jewels flying everywhere, creating a terrible din.

"Burglars!" cried a loud voice from the corridor. "Quick, arrest them!"
"Hide," hissed Lola, dodging behind the plinth. Emelia went behind a curtain and Thea dived under a table. Outside the door, footsteps thundered down the corridor.

Suddenly, soldiers rushed in, followed by the king and queen. "All the jewels are here, Your Highness," reported the Captain.

The queen looked around, smiling. "So where are the thieves?" she asked. Everyone followed her gaze to the pink slippers peeping out from the curtains, the blue skirt sticking out from behind the plinth and the princess curled up under the table.

"Maybe we should lock up the throne room for a week while it's made more secure?" suggested the king. Lola gasped. A week without food? "No!" she cried, jumping out. "Sorry, Daddy, we were just playing."

Thea and Emelia emerged from their hiding places and explained how Lola's nose got stuck in the crown. The king thought it was hilarious.

"I thought you'd be angry," said Lola.

"I'm just relieved you weren't robbers," he laughed. "Why weren't you in bed?"

Lola explained about the midnight feast. "Midnight Feast?" said the king. "What fun. Can we join in?"

"Of course!" cried Lola and she led everyone down to the kitchen to make a feast.

As they tucked in, the king had everyone in fits of laughter as he told them all about the midnight feasts he'd had as a boy. When they'd finished, everyone agreed it had been the best midnight feast, ever. "Would you all like to wear my crown?" the king asked.

"Yes please!" cried the princesses. They all felt so proud as they paraded up and down, wearing the crown, but this time they all made sure it didn't slip down over their noses!

Princess Grace and the Wishing Stone

One day, Princess Grace woke up feeling unusually grumpy. Normally, she was a happy princess, but this particular day she felt tired and very cross, indeed.

"I don't want to!" she cried, when the queen suggested she wore her new, blue dress. "I'm not hungry," she replied, when the king told her to eat up her breakfast. Then, when he told her to stop fidgeting, she announced she was fed up of everyone telling her what to do.

Grace got up and stomped out of the dining room. In fact, she kept on stomping until she reached the door to the old tower. She smiled when she saw it. The tower would be a brilliant place to get away from bossy parents. No-one had been up there for years.

A small, stone staircase led to the top of the tower. There, Grace found an old, wooden door. It was stiff and creaky, but after some pushing, she managed to open it. The door led into a room that was bare, apart from a little rocking chair and a wooden box on a table. "I wonder if there is anything in it?" said Grace, opening the box.

Inside was a shiny, blue stone. Grace picked it up. Underneath, was a note which read, *Be Careful What You Wish For.* She slipped the stone into her pocket and sat in the rocking chair to read her book. How wonderfully peaceful it was.

A little while later, Grace felt hungry. It was nearly time for lunch. She left the tower and walked downstairs. In the palace corridor, she smelt fish and her bad mood returned. Grace wrinkled up her nose in disgust.

"How I wish it was jelly and ice-cream and chocolate cake!" she said, walking into the dining room. Grace stopped and stared. It was! The table was full of bowls of six different colored jellies, seven flavors of ice cream and the biggest chocolate cake she'd ever seen in her life.

Grace sat down and, greedily, began to eat. She ate and ate until she could eat no more and her stomach felt as though it would burst. Groaning, she got down from the table. How her tummy hurt!

Grace spent the whole afternoon lying down, clutching her stomach, feeling sorry for herself. That evening, she'd just started to feel better, when her maid, Anna, came in. Grace scowled. She knew that Anna had come to tell her to go to bed. Well, she didn't feel like it.

"I wish I could stay up late," muttered Grace. Incredibly, Anna turned and walked away.

Later on, when the king and queen looked in on Grace, they didn't tell her to go to bed, either. It was brilliant. So, instead, Grace spent the whole night exploring the castle. At first it was fun, but soon Grace found it boring and quiet with everyone else in bed. She slumped down onto a sofa and soon fell asleep.

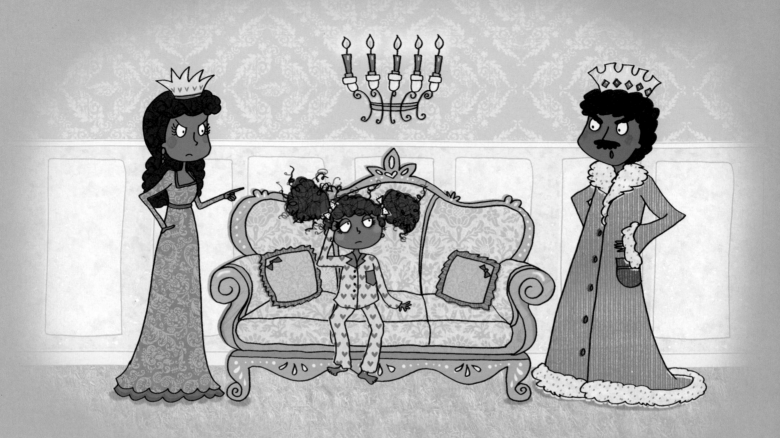

When Grace woke up, the next morning, she was stiff and ached all over. "What are you doing in here, Grace?" asked the queen, crossly. "You should go to sleep in your bed, not on the royal sofas," added the king. "I'm disappointed in you, Grace. Hurry up and get washed before breakfast."

Grace scowled. Everyone was telling her what to do again. She couldn't seem to do anything right. Grace was fed up again. So, she stomped up to the tower to hide once more.

Below, Grace could hear Anna and her mother calling for her. Eventually, she'd have to go down and face them. "I wish I could stay up here forever," she sighed.

Suddenly, there was a whooshing sound. Grace looked around. She walked over to the door, or where the door had been, and stared in amazement. It had disappeared! How could it have gone? Had it moved? Grace looked around for another door, but there was none. Desperately, she felt round the walls for secret buttons that might make them move. There was nothing. Even the window had vanished. There was no way out. Grace would be trapped forever.

"Help!" she cried. "Somebody help me, please!" Grace banged on the window and stamped her feet. "Help! I'm stuck in the tower." However, there was no reply

Grace started to cry. Suddenly, she longed to be back down in the castle with everyone. Her parents weren't horrible, they were actually kind and caring. How mean she'd been to them. Now she couldn't even tell them how sorry she was.

As her tears flowed even more, Grace reached into her pocket for a tissue. Instead, she found the blue stone she'd discovered earlier. Grace recalled the words of the note. *Be Careful What You Wish For.* Everything she'd wished for, the yummy lunch, staying up all night, being in the tower forever, had come true. The blue stone was a magic wishing stone! Grace held it tight and closed her eyes. "I wish I could leave the tower and see my parents," she said.

There was another whooshing sound and the door and window re-appeared. Grace laughed with relief. She flung the door open to find the king and queen standing outside. "We thought we heard you calling," they said. "Is everything alright?"

"Oh, yes," laughed Grace. "Everything is just perfect," and she gave them both a big hug. Then, she went back to the box on the table and put the stone inside. As she did, Grace read the note again and smiled. She'd be very careful what she wished for in future!

A Pet for Princess Polly

It was Princess Polly's birthday and the king said she could have her very own pet. "All you have to decide is what kind of pet you want," said her father, smiling.

Polly was very happy. She had wanted a pet for ages. She was so excited, she giggled and twirled around, clapping her hands. It would be such fun to care for her own pet, to feed it, stroke it and love it. Above all, Polly wanted an animal that would always love her. However, there were so many to choose from. Polly just couldn't make a decision.

The queen smiled as Polly stood there, frowning. "Lots of your friends have pets. Why don't you invite them to come and bring their pets, too," she said. "Maybe that will help you to decide?"

"What a good idea!" said the king. "We will look forward to seeing them."

First, Polly invited Princess Tina over. She lived just over the hill and it wasn't long before she came clip-clopping into the courtyard on her lovely pony, Misty. When Polly saw his shiny coat and his lovely, swishy mane and tail, she was sure she wanted a pony, too. Misty was so beautiful and graceful. Polly couldn't wait to ride him.

Tina helped Polly onto Misty. As she sat on him, Polly felt that she was a long way from the ground. "Giddy up, Misty!" said Tina, and he started to walk.
Then, he began trotting. Bounce, bounce, bounce, went Polly. It was very uncomfortable. "Help!" she cried, but it just made Misty canter. Polly had never been jolted about so much in her life. She felt quite sick. "Stop!" she shouted.

Fortunately, Misty did as he was told and Polly climbed off, shakily. She never wanted to get on a pony again in her life and she certainly didn't want to own one!

"How about a dog?" suggested the queen. "Prince John has a lovely dog. Let's invite them over."

It seemed that Prince John's dog, Rags, thought Princess Polly was his dinner. He bounded up to her, wagging his tail. As Polly backed away, Rags jumped up, putting his two big muddy paws on her shoulders. "Get down!" cried Polly.

"Rags, stop it!" cried Prince John, trying to pull the dog away. Instead of obeying his master, Rags opened his mouth and gave Polly's face a great, big, slobbery, soggy lick! "Yuck!" said Polly, after he'd gone. "I never want to own a dog, ever."
"How about a cat?" asked the king. "Cats don't lick you."

Princess Maisy was always telling Polly what a beautiful, cute, fluffy cat she had and she was delighted to be asked to bring him round the next day. However, to come all that way, Tiger had to travel in a cat box and he hated being boxed in. When Maisy let him out, the angry cat yowled, loudly.

"What a beautiful pussy cat," Polly said, reaching out to stroke him. "Didn't you like it in there, poor thing?"

Tiger glared at her, arched his back and hissed. If Polly hadn't pulled her hand away, quickly, the naughty cat would have scratched her. "I don't want to own a cat, not ever!" cried Polly.

140

The king could see the trouble Polly was having trying to find the perfect pet.
"I have the answer," he said. "How about something small, quiet and easy to look after?"

"Will it bounce me around, or knock me over, or spit at me?" asked Polly.
"No," said the king. "I've already asked Prince Henry to bring his pet, Terence, round."
"But what is Terence?" asked Polly.

The king whispered in Polly's ear and she smiled. Terence sounded perfect. Just then, Prince Henry walked through the palace gates.
"Here he is," he said, holding up a golden cage. " I think Terence is the best pet."

141

Polly opened the cage door and peered inside. "Oh, he's rather hairy," she breathed, gazing at Terence. Just then, the queen called out, "Supper time! Bring your pet, Henry."

As everyone sat down, Henry noticed that the cage door wasn't closed properly. "Oh, dear," he said. "Terence has escaped!"

The king, Henry and Polly quickly began to search the room. "I'd help to look," said the queen, "if you'd tell me what we're looking for?"

Henry looked at her sheepishly. "A tarantula," he replied.
Polly's mother shuddered. "Ugh, it's creepy and crawly. It could be anywhere."
"It's on the back of your dress," said the king. The queen screamed, very loudly.
"There's no way you're having a tarantula for a pet, Polly!" she shrieked and ordered Henry to take Terence home immediately.

Polly didn't want a tarantula either. "All I want is something not too bouncy, or cross, or hairy," she said. "I'd just like a pet that I can sit and cuddle. I can't seem to find one." "I can," said the king, "wait there. I'll be back soon," and he hurried off.

A short time later, the king returned with a white box, wrapped with a pink ribbon. "Happy birthday, Polly," he said, handing it to his daughter.

Polly opened the box. Inside was the cutest, fluffiest rabbit she had ever seen. As he sat on her knee and twitched his little, pink nose, Polly stroked his silky ears. "Thank you," she said. "This really is the perfect pet!"

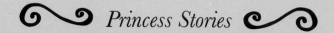

A Proper Princess

It was a lovely, sunny morning. However, Princess Isabella wasn't happy. The dreaded day had come for her to go to Miss Elegant's School for Princesses. Isabella just knew she was going to be a failure. It was the story of her life. Nothing ever went right for her. She couldn't walk elegantly, she couldn't curtsey properly, she couldn't even remember which cutlery to use first at dinner. "I'm just not like how a princess is supposed to be," she sighed.

Isabella jumped out of bed, picked up two books, put them on her head, then walked, slowly, across the room. After three steps, they both fell off. *That's no surprise,* thought the unhappy princess.

Next, Isabella practiced her curtsey. However, she wobbled so much, she almost fell over. She felt like a performing hippo! Finally, Isabella practiced a royal wave and knocked a vase off her shelf. "Maybe, one day, I'll wake up and discover I was swapped at birth," said Isabella. "Maybe I'm not a real princess at all."

"Come on, Isabella!" called her mother, from downstairs. "You should be dressed by now. The coach is setting off for school, soon. How exciting it will be for you to see all your friends again."

Isabella smiled. It would be lovely to see her friends, they were such fun. That was the only good thing about Miss Elegant's school. She was useless at every single lesson.

As Isabella arrived at school, it seemed that everyone was more excited than usual. Princess Lucinda and Princess Angelina rushed up as Isabella climbed out of her coach. "Isabella, how wonderful to see you!" they cried. "Have you heard the news? The best pupils in each class are going to be invited to the Royal Garden Party and be introduced to Prince Oliver."

Isabella sighed. Prince Oliver was the dreamiest prince in the whole of the world. She'd love to be introduced to him. Of course, there was no way she was going to be the best in her class at anything, except doing everything wrong. Isabella was brilliant at that.

As lessons began, everyone tried hard to impress Miss Elegant. "Right, class," she said. "Let's start with riding your ponies in a ladylike manner."

Isabella frowned. She found balancing, elegantly, on ponies very hard. She climbed onto her pony, Silver. Then, she started to trot. Silver was very bouncy. "Oh, no!" cried Isabella. The saddle was beginning to move. Suddenly, she landed with a bump on the ground.

"Are you all right?" asked Miss Elegant.
"Yes, but I just can't ride!" cried Isabella, getting up.

Miss Elegant reassured her that she'd merely forgotten to tighten Silver's girth properly. "It's nothing a bit of practice won't fix," she said. "Always believe in yourself, Isabella," said Miss Elegant. "Never give up. Trying your best is half the battle."

At curtseying class, Isabella tried to curtsey, but she wobbled and fell over.
"Right foot behind, girls," said Miss Elegant. She smiled at Isabella. "You can do it.
Remember, believe you can and you will."
I can do it thought Isabella, as she curtsied again. Amazingly, she did it without falling
over. However, the waltz class was hard work and Isabella panicked. She didn't know
which foot went where. "Ouch!" cried Angelina, as Isabella stood on her toe.
"Back with the left foot first, Isabella," said Miss Elegant. "Remember, you can do it."

"Back on the left foot," Isabella whispered to herself. "I can do it!" Amazingly, she did.
Isabella continued to believe as she practiced hard. Soon, she felt more confident than
she ever had done before.

Isabella even got better at walking elegantly, sitting down gracefully and making polite conversation. She still felt that every other princess was still better than her.

When Miss Elegant called the class together to announce who was going to the royal garden party, everyone else was bursting with excitement. "For their all round princess like accomplishments, I have chosen Angelina and Lucinda," said Miss Elegant, smiling. "Yippeee!" cried Angelina and Lucinda, dancing around in a most unprincess-like fashion.

Miss Elegant held up her hand for silence. "There is one extra place at the garden party," she said. "Because she has tried so hard and is the most improved princess of all, Isabella will also attend."

Everyone clapped and cheered. Isabella smiled, amazed. She couldn't quite believe it!

Finally, the big day arrived. Carefully, Isabella put on her best dress and checked that her hair looked perfect. She walked, elegantly, and she sat down, gracefully. Isabella remembered to say, "I can do it," if she was unsure about something.

As she mingled with the other guests, Isabella thought that the garden party was even more wonderful than she'd dreamed. Feeling more nervous than ever, she waited to be introduced to the prince.

Miss Elegant watched Isabella and knew that she was beginning to believe in herself.

Suddenly, Isabella's name was called out. Her big moment had come. This is what she had been practicing for. Was she going to mess it up?

Isabella curtsied, daintily, and didn't fall over. She even laughed, prettily, at Prince Oliver's jokes. Then, later, Prince Oliver chose Isabella for the opening dance at the ball, Miss Elegant nearly had kittens. Surely Isabella would step on his toes, or trip over her feet? However, she didn't. She danced beautifully. In fact, she so impressed Prince Oliver, that he danced with her nearly all evening. It seemed to Isabella, and everyone else there, that she was a proper princess after all.

A Royal Adventure

King Andrew frowned as he hurried out of the palace. It was a Sunday, but, as always, work was more important than fun. Just then, Prince Harold cantered up on his pony, Moonlight. "Look at me! Look at me!" he cried.

King Andrew didn't hear him and jumped into the royal carriage. Prince Harold frowned. His dad was always too busy to spend time with him and his sister, Jemima. Well, he'd make him stop, if only for a minute. "I'm jumping the gate!" he yelled.

Princess Jemima looked up from the picture she was painting for her father's birthday. She watched, horrified, as Moonlight raced towards the gate and then suddenly stopped. Harold kept going, right over Moonlight's head, landing in a heap on the other side of the gate.

"Oh, dear, are you all right?" cried Jemima.
Harold picked himself up and turned to see if his father had noticed. However, the royal carriage was disappearing, in a cloud of dust, down the drive. "I thought we were going to have lunch!" cried Harold. "I'm sorry," called the king from the carriage. "I've got an urgent meeting."

Jemima sighed. Their father always had meetings. She went back to painting the picture. At least he'd spend time with them on his birthday, tomorrow. He'd promised they'd go on a boat trip and Jemima was really looking forward to it.

The next day, Jemima got up early to give the king his present and card, but couldn't find him. So, she went into the garden to look. "Mind out!" cried Harold, who was shooting arrows at a target. One of them only just missed Jemima's head!

"What are you doing?" she asked. "You should be careful with those arrows."
"I have to practice," replied Harold. "I'm doing an archery show for Dad's birthday treat. I'm practicing getting a bull's-eye."

Jemima smiled. Harold's show sounded really exciting. She was useless at sport, but she was better than him at reading and painting pictures. Jemima glanced down at the picture she had painted of her father's horse. It had taken her days, but she was so proud of it. "What's that?" laughed Harold, "It looks like a crooked old donkey."

"It's Dad's horse," said Jemima. "I painted it for his birthday."
Harold sneered. "You're always wasting your time messing around with paints and reading. What use are they to anyone?"

Jemima felt hurt. To her, pictures and books made life more beautiful. Harold was always showing off, trying to make himself look better than her. She hoped her father didn't think her present was useless.

Suddenly, the king came striding along. "Happy Birthday, Daddy!" cried Jemima, rushing up to him. "I've got a present and card for you. I made them myself."
"Oh, how lovely, darling," said the king, looking at them, quickly. "I'm really sorry, but I've got to go out now."

The queen stopped the king at the door. "Your children were looking forward to having fun with you on your birthday," she said. "You should be with them."
"I'm sorry, I just haven't got time," replied the king. "I'll be back for my birthday dinner, tonight, though." With that, the king dashed off.

Jemima and Harold were really upset. "Don't worry, we'll all have fun tonight," said the queen, in a reassuring voice. "We'll have a lovely dinner and you can spend all the time you like with your Dad."

So, Jemima and Harold waited, excitedly, for the king to come home. However, the hours dragged by and still he didn't come. In the end, they had dinner without him.

"Dad couldn't even get back for my archery show," sighed Harold, as they went to bed. "Nothing we do will ever be good enough to get his attention."
Just for once, Jemima had to agree with her brother.

The palace was still and quiet as everyone slept in their beds.
Then, suddenly, at midnight, Jemima and Harold were woken by a crashing sound, downstairs. Harold sat up in bed. "That sounds like a window being broken," he said. "I think there are burglars downstairs."
"Come on," whispered Jemima. "We must stop them. Bring your bow and arrows. Quick!"

Together, they tip-toed downstairs to see two men heading towards the door. One was carrying the crown jewels and the other had the king's birthday presents. "I'll distract them while you stop them with your arrows!" Jemima hissed. She darted along the hall and hid behind a statue. "Oooooh," she wailed. "Ooooooh!"

The burglars froze. Behind them, Harold loaded an arrow into his bow and he took aim.

Whoosh! The arrow flew through the air and whizzed past one burglar's nose, hitting the dinner gong, making it bong loudly. "Aaargh!" he cried, dropping the crown jewels with a clatter. "What was that? This place is haunted."

Meanwhile, Jemima climbed, quietly, behind a small suit of armor. The two robbers were yelling so much, they didn't even notice her. "Get out!" yelled one. "Quick!"

"We can't leave without the crown jewels!" cried the other, dropping the king's birthday presents and rushing back to pick up the stolen goods. The first robber, however, didn't care about anything but getting out.

As he ran past Jemima, she cleverly made the suit of armor move. "Stop," Jemima cried, in the gruffest voice she could manage. The thief shrieked and whirled round so fast, he fell over.
The other robber was so startled, he dropped all the crown jewels, again. Before he could pick them all up, Harold was standing over him, pointing his bow and arrow down at him. "Don't move!" he yelled.

Meanwhile, Jemima waved her arm up and down again. The masked robber thought the armor was alive! "Please don't hurt me!" he begged.

All the noise woke the king and queen up. They came running downstairs and called the guard. Soon, the burglars were arrested. "I can't believe you two stopped those robbers all on your own!" said the queen, hugging her children. "How clever of you!"

"How did you do it?" asked. the king, looking amazed.
"Harold was brilliant at archery," said Jemima.
"It was all Jemima's clever plan!" Harold grinned.
"You're inventive and you've got sporting skills!" said the king. "What a good team you make." He shook his head and smiled. "I never knew my children were so clever."
"That's because you're too busy to know them at all," said the queen.

The king put his arm round each of his children. "Well, from now on, I'm going to spend time getting to know them both," he said. "Let's start with a midnight feast!"

Harold and Jemima cheered. At last, they had got their father's attention.
Now they were going to have a midnight feast. It was the perfect end to a very busy day!